Sylvie
and the
Wolf

ANDREA DEBBINK

Illustrated by Mercè López

sounds true
BOULDER, COLORADO

For my Rose Sylvie.
And to aunts and uncles everywhere.
—A.D.

For Erica and Ania, who have walked
with me through this illustrated forest.
—M.L.

Sounds True
Boulder, CO 80306

Text © 2023 Andrea Debbink
Illustrations © 2023 Mercè López

Published 2023

Book design by Ranée Kahler

Printed in China

BK06322

Library of Congress Cataloging-in-Publication Data

Names: Debbink, Andrea, author. | López, Mercè, 1979- illustrator.
Title: Sylvie and the Wolf / by Andrea Debbink ; illustrated by Merce
   Lopez.
Description: Boulder, CO : Sounds True, 2023. | Audience: Ages 4-8.
Identifiers: LCCN 2022010673 (print) | LCCN 2022010674 (ebook) | ISBN
   9781683648697 (hardback) | ISBN 9781683648703 (ebook)
Subjects: CYAC: Fear—Fiction. | LCGFT: Picture books.
Classification: LCC PZ7.1.D39885 Sy 2023 (print) | LCC PZ7.1.D39885
   (ebook) | DDC [E]—dc23
LC record available at https://lccn.loc.gov/2022010673
LC ebook record available at https://lccn.loc.gov/2022010674

10 9 8 7 6 5 4 3 2 1

High in the mountains,
where shadow meets light,
lived a girl named Sylvie.

Sylvie was not afraid of anything.

Not the brooding forest
that crept to the edge of the town.

Not the twisting paths
and wild streams.

She dreamed of the day she'd
    climb the mountains,
and imagined the wider world.

Sylvie was not afraid
    of anything—
until she met the Wolf.

The fog made deep shadows that day.
The snow broke under Sylvie's boots,
and the branches creaked above.
But everything else was silent
and still.

Until one of the shadows *moved*.

Sylvie saw the sweep of a tail,
the gleam of eyes, the glint of teeth.
She heard a growl.

Her heart flapped like a bird,
and she had one loud thought:
WOLF!

Sylvie ran.

Back at home, Tante asked,
"Sylvie? What's wrong?"
But safe by Tante's side,
the answer seemed foolish
and Sylvie couldn't say it.
Wolves lived in fairy tales and
faraway lands, not here.

The Wolf became Sylvie's secret.

He seemed to be everywhere she went.
His shadow lurked in the village streets.
His footprints appeared on the distant hills.
And he growled in the grove where the old owl slept.

Sylvie stopped exploring.
Her world became small.

But secrets are heavy
and are hard to carry alone.

Sylvie told a friend about the Wolf.
Her secret spread.

"Wolf?" the other children laughed.
"No one's ever seen a wolf in our forest!"

Sylvie knew better.

So when her friends said,
"Come skate with us!"
Sylvie said, "Not today."

And when the neighbors
had a bonfire,
Sylvie stayed home.

Finally one day, Sylvie didn't want
to leave the house at all.

When Tante asked,
"Sylvie, what's wrong?"
Sylvie knew it was time to tell her
    about the Wolf.

Tante did not laugh.

"Maybe we should see if there are any
    wolves in our forest," she said.
"Maybe you can find out?"
    Sylvie asked.
"Maybe we can go together,"
    Tante said.

Snow fell like sifted sugar.

They explored the town streets.
No shadow.

They hiked to the tops of the distant hills.
No footprints.

And they wandered the grove where the old owl slept,
but there wasn't a sound.

As they crossed the meadow toward home,
they heard a howl.

It came from their old woodshed.

Tante and Sylvie stopped to listen.
Then Tante did something odd: she whistled.
A howl came through the door
and it was followed by—

the Wolf!

Sylvie saw the sweep of a tail,
the gleam of eyes,
the glint of teeth.

But she also saw something else.

The animal was no wolf at all.

"A dog?" Sylvie asked.
"A very frightened dog," Tante said.

The dog stayed hidden in the woodshed.

Day after day, Tante and Sylvie left food by the woodshed door.
Finally one day, Sylvie was brave enough to do it alone.

She set down the food
and waited.

She heard a scuffle.
Her heart flapped and her legs trembled,
but she did not run.

The dog stared at Sylvie.
Sylvie stared back.

And then,

she knew.

"Rune?"

Rune had been Sylvie's puppy when
she was a small child.

But he had run away long ago,
spooked by something since forgotten.
Alone in the shadowy places,
he became wild and skittish.

Courage would take time—
and practice.

Sometimes Rune would still howl in the
night for no reason at all.
Sometimes Sylvie would wake up and forget
that she didn't still have a secret.